Are You Empathetic Today?

Five Points
Pet Shelter

FERNE PRESS

Written by Kris Yankee and Marian Nelson • Illustrated by Jeff Covieo

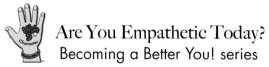

Are You Empathetic Today?
Becoming a Better You! series

Copyright © 2014 by Kris Yankee and Marian Nelson

Layout and cover design by Jacqueline L. Challiss Hill
Illustrations by Jeff Covieo
Illustrations created with digital graphics

Printed in Canada

Summary: Kids learn ways to be empathetic toward others.
Library of Congress Cataloging-in-Publication Data
Yankee, Kris and Nelson, Marian
Are You Empathetic Today?/Kris Yankee and Marian Nelson–First Edition
ISBN-13: 978-1-938326-26-4
1. Empathy. 2. Self-esteem. 3. Character education. 4. Self-assurance. 5. Respect. 6. Confidence.
I. Yankee, Kris and Nelson, Marian II. Title
Library of Congress Control Number: 2014949855

FERNE PRESS

Ferne Press is an imprint of Nelson Publishing & Marketing
366 Welch Road, Northville, MI 48167
www.nelsonpublishingandmarketing.com
(248) 735-0418

More Praise for *Are You Empathetic Today?*

Dedication

This book is dedicated to all of the great role models, parents, educators, and individuals who are committed to building healthy character in people of all ages. It is because of your loyalty to humanity that we will see the lasting results in our children. They will grow up to be positive role models for the next generation.

A special thank you to the staff at Nelson Publishing & Marketing, Kathy Dyer, Amanda Clothier, Jacqueline Hill, and Jennifer Lenders, for their ideas, suggestions, support, and vision for the future.

Every day is a new day.

Today is about being empathetic.

When you are empathetic,
you are understanding, aware, and sensitive to others' feelings.

Try this!

Each day when you wake up, say out loud,

"I am going to be aware of how others feel."

Helping your brother do his chores
makes the job easier for him and takes less time.
Noticing that he needs help is showing empathy.

"Thanks!"

A friend tells you that he lost his pet.
Even if this hasn't happened to you,
you know how sad he feels just by looking at his face.
You feel bad for him.

When the librarian has a cart full of books,
you and your friend give her a helping hand.

After you receive a
low grade on an assignment,
you may feel as if you're
the only one who
has ever done poorly.

Your teacher is understanding and willing to help you improve.

When a new classmate arrives in the middle of the school year, you know how she feels since you've had to move before. You'll stick by her and help her learn about the classroom.

It's such a relief to know that new classmates
are helpful and friendly.

Helping someone new in school is a great way to show empathy.

"She's really
nice!"

You can help your friend with his lunch because you know how hard it is to get around when you have an injury.

Sometimes helping out can be difficult, but it's worth it when you can make a difference for someone.

Wow! You really care!

If you haven't learned to be empathetic,
you may not know how important it is to be understanding,
aware, and sensitive to other people's feelings.

Find out more about what's happening and then do the right thing.

"See? We have glasses
and braces, too!"

Sometimes Grandma tells you the same story more than once. Listen patiently because she might tell you something new that you'll need to remember.

Donating your toys to kids who might not have any is a good way to show empathy toward others.

"Am I going to play with these anymore?"

KEEP

DONATE

A good friend can tell when you're feeling sad.

She *wants* to listen and try to help you.

When we participate in a service project,
we are aware and understanding of the needs
in our community.

When a teammate makes an error,
you know exactly how he feels.

Even if you've won the game,
you understand that the other team's players feel bad about losing.
You offer a sincere "good game" and a handshake.

You are a good sport!

Decide to start today.
Notice how others are feeling and be understanding
and aware of what's going on in their lives.

Having empathy in our hearts affects how we treat each other and can make the world a better place.

"Thanks for coming!"

Now you know why we all need to show empathy.
Life is happier and more fulfilling with an empathetic heart.

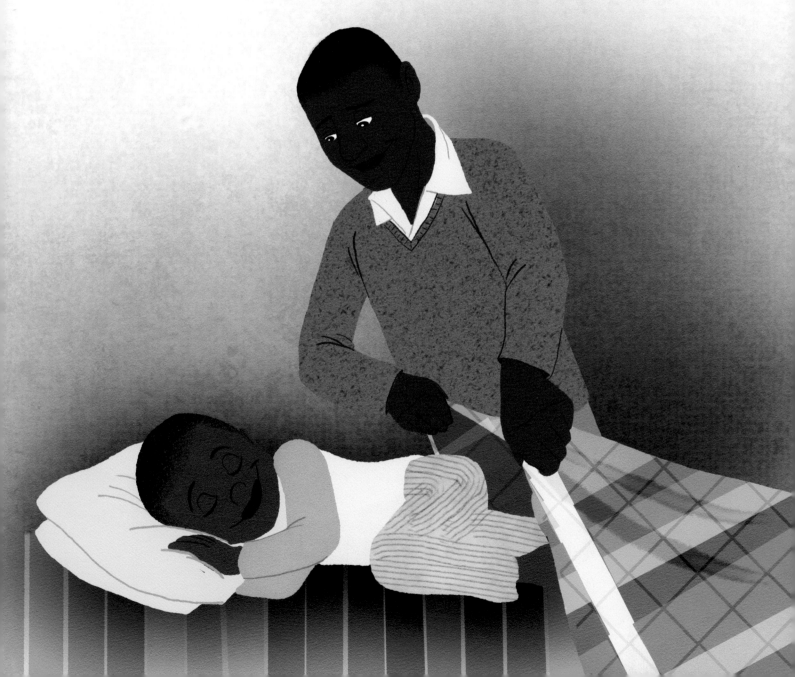

When you lay your head down on your pillow tonight,
think about all of the ways you felt empathetic
and those times you showed kindness to others.

Give yourself
a big hug.

Reflections

- Name four times when you were aware of how someone else was feeling.
- What do you do if someone is making fun of one of your friends?
- What do you do when you've made a mistake and hurt someone's feelings?
- Have you ever excluded someone from playing, from a class project, or from the lunch table? What could you have done differently?
- What do you do when someone tells you the same story over and over again? Do you listen, or are you rude?
- Have you ever been an observer in nature? Sit outside and watch the birds, insects, and other animals around you. How many creatures did you see?
- Name three ways to show empathy toward a pet.
- How has someone been empathetic toward you? Name two times.
- How can you remember to be more empathetic to the lunch lady or custodian at school?
- If someone is crying, how would you show that you care?
- Have you ever been on a losing team? How did you feel when you were teased for losing? What could the winning opponents have said differently? Remember that for yourself the next time you're on the winning team.
- If a friend is afraid to try something new, what words could you say to help him/her?
- What are ways to show you really care about another person?
- Empathy is a feeling you have in your heart. How we respond to others is the action we take. If your friend is sad and hurting, you will feel a sense of sadness, too. Name a time that this has happened.
- Sometimes just listening to a friend is what is needed. You may want to jump in and fix the problem, but stop yourself and wait. A good friend can be a good listener, too. Name a time that you jumped in instead of waiting.
- If someone tells you something that is personal to him/her and asks you not to repeat it, it is your responsibility to not gossip about what has been told to you. Just think of how you would feel if someone told something about you that was personal. It hurts. Remember how that felt. Name a time that has happened to you. Trust is very important.

Tips for Creating Empathetic Kids

- Provide empathy opportunities: visit a shut-in relative, volunteer at a food pantry or an animal shelter, make "Get Well" cards for friends and relatives.
- Empathy is not always about being sad. Take a look at the front cover—the kids have a sense of fulfillment and inner happiness because they are helping take care of unwanted animals. Express to kids that empathy can sometimes bring you joyful feelings, not just sad ones.
- Saying "I'm sorry" is a great way to mend someone's heart that's been hurt. Another more impactful way is to make an "I'm sorry" card.
- Empathy can be a learned behavior. Be sure to be an excellent role model for those in your care by showing that you understand, are aware of, and are sensitive to how they are feeling.
- Empathy sometimes looks like "helping" but it really isn't. An empathetic person is keenly observant of what is going on around him/her. Play a game with your child to see who can observe the most of what's happening in a given environment (i.e., neighborhood, park, playground, etc.).
- Encourage kids to be respectful and empathetic toward siblings and friends. Create a family mission about how people should treat each other. Make the pledge to uphold that mission.
- Being aware of those less fortunate is important because it helps us relate to humanity. Do kind acts such as donating clothing and household items. Rather than throwing these items in the trash, identify those who could benefit from them.
- Modeling empathetic and caring actions toward others makes you feel good about yourself. Help kids understand this win-win situation.
- Developing empathy toward family members creates a happier home. These behaviors will then extend to the world outside, thus creating a happier world.
- Take time every day to show you care about your loved ones.
- Kids are sponges; they watch how adults treat each other. Exhibit behavior that reflects care and respect wherever you are.

Dear Reader,

Why is empathy so important? Kids are growing up in a technological age that enables them to spend more time with "screen" friends than "real" friends. This lack of face-to-face communication diminishes empathy opportunities. A lack of empathy then leads to a lack of communication skills, a lack of respect for others, and a rise in selfishness.

To develop empathy, we need to center ourselves on our hearts. If the heart is left out, there will be more people who act without feeling. Any time you leave out feeling, there is a huge lack of caring. What happens when people don't care about each other? Anger, rage, and destruction occur. It is vital to connect head, hands, and heart in order to develop the character of a person to his/her highest potential.

This is our goal with this series of books. We are sure you would agree that as a parent, teacher, caregiver, or administrator that we need to strive for the same goal.

Kris Yankee and Marian Nelson

Author Biographies

Photo by Eric Yankee

Kris Yankee is the co-founder of High 5 for Character, as well as an editor, writer, and mom. The values presented by High 5 for Character and this new series are those that she and her husband hope to instill in their two children. She is an award-winning author of several titles.
Visit krisyankee.com or find Kris on Facebook and Twitter.

For nearly ten years, Marian Nelson has been the publisher for Nelson Publishing & Marketing with over 165 titles in print. As a veteran educator, Marian keeps her focus on the children of the world, actively pursuing concepts that build healthy character. It is her hope that people will continue to learn, grow, and be inspired by all of the books that we publish. Visit nelsonpublishingandmarketing.com to see the wide variety of subject matter.

Photo by Eric Yankee

Visit us at high5forcharacter.com.
Like us at facebook.com/High5ForCharacter   Follow us on Twitter @Hi5ForCharacter

Illustrator Biography

Jeff Covieo has been drawing since he could hold a pencil and hasn't stopped since. He has a BFA in photography from College for Creative Studies in Michigan and works in the commercial photography field, though drawing and illustration have been his avocation for years. *Are You Empathetic Today?* is the tenth book he has illustrated.